PUF

Gyles Brandreth was born in ... versity in 1970 with a degree ... has had a busy and varied care... ...more than fifty books published on a whole range of topics. He has also written television scripts and is a well-known broadcaster. Gyles is the founder of the Teddy Bear Museum in Stratford-upon-Avon and the chairman of the National Playing Fields Association, the charity that protects and improves playgrounds and play space throughout the United Kingdom. Gyles became the Member of Parliament for Chester in 1992.

By the same author

GYLES BRANDRETH

THE HULLABALOO AT NO. 13

ILLUSTRATED BY LYNNE BYRNES

PUFFIN BOOKS

PUFFIN BOOKS

Published by the Penguin Group
Penguin Books Ltd, 27 Wrights Lane, London W8 5TZ, England
Penguin Books USA Inc., 375 Hudson Street, New York, New York 10014, USA
Penguin Books Australia Ltd, Ringwood, Victoria, Australia
Penguin Books Canada Ltd, 10 Alcorn Avenue, Toronto, Ontario, Canada M4V 3B2
Penguin Books (NZ) Ltd, 182–190 Wairau Road, Auckland 10, New Zealand

Penguin Books Ltd, Registered Offices: Harmondsworth, Middlesex, England

First published by Viking 1992
Published in Puffin Books 1993
1 3 5 7 9 10 8 6 4 2

Text copyright © Gyles Brandreth, 1992
Illustrations copyright © Lynne Byrnes, 1992
All rights reserved

The moral right of the author has been asserted

Filmset in Palatino
Printed in England by Clays Ltd, St Ives plc

1. A Secret at No. 13

Hamlet Orlando Julius Caesar Brown had a problem. And it wasn't his name. It was the lion that was about to eat him.

The lion was pounding down the High Street, roaring as he came. Hamlet stood stock-still, trembling, terrified, unable to scream, and now, as the huge animal put his massive paws on Hamlet's shoulders, unable to move.

The lion opened his gigantic jaws. He snarled and showed his ferocious teeth.

Then with his big, hard, rough tongue, the king of beasts licked the nine-year-old boy on the nose. And that's when Hamlet woke up.

And that, too, was when Hamlet Orlando Julius Caesar Brown realized he had another problem. And it wasn't a lion. It was a puppy, a large, snuffly, wet-nosed puppy, sitting on

Hamlet's pillow licking Hamlet's face.

Hamlet pinched himself. This wasn't a dream, but in a way it was a dream come true. Hamlet had always wanted a puppy of his own and here was one, as large as life, as friendly as could be, and behaving as though it felt very much at home.

It couldn't be a Christmas present because it was only the fifteenth of December. And it wouldn't be a Christmas present anyway, because pets were banned in the Brown household.

Hamlet lived at No. 13 Irving Terrace, Hammersmith, West London, with his mother, his father, his goodie-goodie eleven-year-old sister, Susan, and a goldfish called Spot.

"A goldfish isn't a proper pet," said Hamlet. "You can't have any fun with him."

"It's not a him, it's a her," said Susan.

"I hate know-alls," said Hamlet rudely. "Anyway, I don't care if it's a him or a her, it's stupid. It can't even remember its own name."

"That's because a goldfish's memory only

lasts for thirty seconds," said Susan.

"That's interesting," said Mrs Brown.

"That's boring," said Hamlet. "What I'd like to have is a puppy. That's my idea of a proper pet."

Mr Brown said, "Puppies grow into dogs and a dog's a big responsibility."

Mrs Brown said, "Puppies make messes and I know who would have to clear up those messes!"

Susan Brown said, "I prefer cats."

Hamlet Brown said, "I want a puppy!"

And now he had one. Yippee! thought Hamlet. The puppy made a snuffling noise and wagged his tail happily.

How had the puppy arrived? Hamlet's bedroom door was closed, but his window was open. Could the puppy have climbed through the window in the middle of the night? Hamlet got up and went over to the window. Yes, there were dirty paw marks on the window-ledge. The bold little puppy must

have run along the garden wall and jumped on to the roof of the extension that was just outside Hamlet's window.

"You're quite a mountaineer," said Hamlet, patting the puppy gently on the head. The puppy wagged his tail in agreement.

Who does he belong to? Hamlet thought to himself. Then out loud he said, "He belongs to *me*!"

There was a noise on the landing. It was Susan going down to breakfast.

"You belong to *me*," Hamlet whispered to the puppy. "And this is going to be your new home." The puppy made a little woof sound.

"Don't make too much noise. This has got to be our secret. No one must know you are here. Do you understand?"

"Woof! Woof!" growled the puppy, a bit too loudly.

From the kitchen Mr Brown called, "Hamlet, what is going on up there?"

2. Puppy Love

It was Saturday morning, and at No. 13 on a Saturday morning, Mr Brown always made the family a cooked breakfast, and Mrs Brown always stayed in bed till ten o'clock, wearing eye-shades and ear-plugs so she wouldn't be disturbed.

Mr Brown was an actor. That's how Hamlet Orlando Julius Caesar Brown got his unusual names. They were the names of characters Mr Brown had played on stage in the year that Hamlet was born. Mrs Brown was an actor too. The Christmas before Susan was born, Mr and Mrs Brown had acted together in *Aladdin*. Mr Brown had played Aladdin's wicked uncle, Abanazar, and Mrs Brown had been the beautiful Princess Badroulboudour.

"Badroulboudour is a lovely name for a girl," Mr Brown had said at the time.

"Nonsense," said Mrs Brown, which is how their daughter came to be named after Mrs Brown's sister, Susan.

Mrs Brown didn't act on the stage any more, but Mr Brown did. This Christmas he was going to be playing the part of Buttons in the pantomime *Cinderella*.

This morning he was cooking breakfast in the kitchen at No. 13. And what a breakfast it was: scrambled eggs, baked beans, mushrooms, bacon, tinned tomatoes, masses of hot buttered toast, and hot chocolate with at least two inches of whipped cream squirted on top.

Susan was already at the table. Susan was never late for breakfast. Susan was never late for anything.

Hamlet left his bedroom and came clattering down the stairs into the kitchen.

"What's going on up there, my boy?" said Mr Brown, raising a suspicious eyebrow at his son.

"Nothing," said Hamlet. "Sorry I'm late."

"In fact, you're just in time," said Mr Brown, passing his son a plate piled high with food.

As Hamlet took his place at the table, from upstairs there came a noise – a bang, then a yap, then a scratching sound.

"What was that?" said Susan.

"Nothing," said Hamlet, suddenly talking rather loudly.

"I'm sure I heard something," said Susan.

"This is delicious," said Hamlet, ignoring his sister. "Can I have some more bacon, please?"

"Of course," said Mr Brown.

Two minutes later, Hamlet said, "Can I have a bit more bacon, please?"

"By all means," said Mr Brown.

Five minutes later, Hamlet asked, "There isn't any more bacon, is there?"

"Goodness!" exclaimed Mr Brown, who had now run out of bacon. "What's he doing with it?"

"He's stuffing it into his pockets, that's what," said Susan.

"Sneak," snapped Hamlet.

"It's true," said Susan.

"Children, children, stop it!" said Mr Brown. "Will somebody tell me what is going on?"

"Hamlet's putting all the bacon into his pockets."

"Don't be silly, Susan, he can't be."

"He is."

"Are you, Hamlet?" asked Mr Brown, wide-eyed with amazement.

Hamlet didn't know what to say. He didn't dare tell his father he had put the bacon in his pocket to take to his puppy for breakfast, so instead he said, "I don't like bacon."

"You liked bacon last Saturday," said Mr Brown.

"I don't like it now."

"Then why did you ask for more?"

Hamlet couldn't think of what to say, so he didn't say anything. He wanted to cry. Instead he pulled the five bits of bacon out of his pocket and put them back on his plate.

"I think you're up to something, Hamlet Brown," said Mr Brown sternly. "I'm going to have to keep a close eye on you, my boy."

There was another noise from upstairs.

"What's that?" said Mr Brown.

"It's just Mum," said Hamlet, and it was.

"She doesn't sound as if she's in a very good mood," said Susan.

Susan was right as usual. Mrs Brown was in a very bad mood. She was coming downstairs, calling in a very cross voice, "Hamlet, Susan, come here at once. *At once!*"

The children ran into the hallway, quickly followed by Mr Brown. "What's all the hullabaloo about, my sweet?"

"What's this?" shrieked Mrs Brown.

"What's what, my sweet?" cooed Mr Brown.

"That's what!" cried Mrs Brown, pointing to a large puddle at the foot of the stairs.

"It's –"

"I know what it is," exclaimed Mrs Brown.

"What I want to know is how it got there."

"I did it," said Hamlet all of a sudden.

Everybody had been looking at the puddle.
It was a very large puddle. Now everyone
turned and looked at Hamlet.

"You did it?" said Mrs Brown.

"You can't have done!" said Mr Brown.

Susan giggled.

"It's all Susan's fault!" said Hamlet. "She was in the loo. I couldn't help it."

"Hamlet, you are nine years old. I don't believe what I'm hearing," said Mrs Brown.

"Nor do I," said Mr Brown.

"I know who did it," said Susan.

"No you don't," said Hamlet.

"Yes I do," said Susan. "He did it!" And she pointed to the little puppy who was sitting at the top of the stairs, wagging his tail.

"Good gracious," said Mr Brown. "It's a puppy."

"He's a beagle by the look of him," said Mrs Brown. "What on earth is he doing here?"

"He's mine!" said Hamlet.

"No he's not," said Susan.

"Will you two stop this at once," said Mrs Brown fiercely, "and tell me exactly what's going on."

3. Puddles is Perfect

Hamlet told his story: how he had woken up
and found the puppy on his pillow, how he
had realized the puppy must have climbed
through the window in the night, how he
must have forgotten to shut his bedroom door
properly when he came down for breakfast,
how he had tried to take the puppy some
bacon for his breakfast.

"Well," said Mr Brown when Hamlet had
finished, "what are we going to do now?"

"We're going to keep him," said Hamlet.
"Aren't we?"

"No, we're not," said Mrs Brown, who was
fetching a bucket and mop.

"Why not, Mum? *Please*."

"He is very sweet," said Susan, who was
now patting the puppy on the head, much to
Hamlet's disgust.

"For a start, he isn't house-trained," said Mrs Brown. "And secondly, he isn't ours."

"I'd better inform the police," said Mr Brown.

"The police!" cried Hamlet. "I didn't steal him. He climbed in through my window."

"Dad isn't going to report you to the police, stupid," said Susan. "He's going to tell the police we've found a puppy."

"Somebody could be very worried because

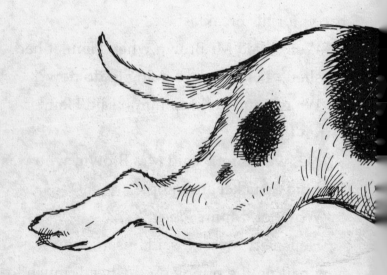

they've lost their pet beagle," explained Mr
Brown. "Are you sure he's a beagle, my
sweet? He looks more like a basset-hound to
me."

"He's a beagle," said Mrs Brown. "He looks
a proper pedigree animal, about twelve weeks
old, I'd say." Mrs Brown knew a lot about
dogs. Mrs Brown knew a lot about most
things.

"A pedigree, eh?" said Mr Brown. "That

means he could be valuable. There might even be a reward. Let's get down to the police station right away.''

Mr Brown and Hamlet and Susan and the puppy set off for the police station by car. Susan and Hamlet had both wanted to carry the puppy.

"He's mine,'' said Hamlet.

"No he isn't,'' said Susan.

"Well, he isn't yours anyway,'' said Hamlet grumpily.

Mr Brown tried to keep the peace by suggesting that Susan carry him there and Hamlet carry him back.

"But what happens if the police have found his owner and he doesn't come back with us?'' said Hamlet. "He came through my window. I should carry him.''

"All right,'' said Mr Brown, who didn't like children who squabbled. "Hamlet gets to carry him there, and if he comes back, it's Susan's turn. Everybody happy?''

They weren't happy, and they were both about to say so, when a very fierce Mr Brown said, "Stop it, you two, and do as your father says."

During the drive to the police station nobody said much. The puppy loved the journey. He spent most of it standing on Hamlet's lap with his front paws against the window, watching the world go by.

Hamlet and Susan had never been into a police station before. They were a little nervous. When they arrived at the front door and saw a large poster of a horrible-looking man who was "WANTED FOR ARMED ROBBERY", they became quite frightened.

"Nothing to worry about here," said Mr Brown, who felt very much at home because he had twice played the part of a policeman on television. "In we go."

Immediately inside the entrance to the police station was a small room with a counter along one side. Standing behind the counter was a policeman, eating a sandwich.

"Good afternoon, officer," said Mr Brown very loudly. "I can guess what you've got in that sandwich."

"What?" said the policeman, taken by surprise.

"Truncheon meat!" said Mr Brown with a laugh.

"Oh, Dad!" moaned Hamlet and Susan.

"Just my little joke," said Mr Brown, winking at the policeman.

"Yes, sir," he replied. "Now what can I do for you?"

"Exhibit number one, coming up!" said Mr Brown, turning to Hamlet who was holding the puppy. "Hamlet, would you please show Hammersmith's very own Sherlock Holmes our own answer to the Hound of the Baskervilles."

Hamlet didn't know what his father was talking about, nor did the policeman.

"Hamlet," said Susan, "put the puppy on the counter."

Hamlet did as he was told.

"Well," said Mr Brown, "what do you think?"

"It's a very nice dog, sir, but we don't use beagles as police dogs as a rule."

"No, no, no, officer," said Mr Brown. "You don't understand. This dog is lost. We've found him and we've brought him to you."

"As a present?" asked the policeman, who was getting quite confused.

"I don't seem to be making myself clear," said Mr Brown with a sigh.

"What my dad is trying to say is, has anyone reported a missing dog?" said Susan.

"Oh," said the policeman, "why didn't you say so?"

"I thought I did," said Mr Brown, "but never mind."

"That's easy," said the policeman. And from under the counter, he produced a large book marked "Lost and Found". He opened it and ran his finger down two or three pages. "How long is it since you found him?"

"I found him this morning," said Hamlet.

"But he could have been missing for months or years," said Mr Brown.

"I doubt that, sir," said the policeman. "He's just a puppy."

"Of course he is. And I'm just an idiot,

aren't I?'' muttered Mr Brown.

The policeman was too polite to answer, and went on looking through the book. "No," he said finally, "nearest thing to it is a poodle that went missing in Shepherd's Bush in November."

"What are we going to do?" said Susan.

"I'm going to keep him," said Hamlet.

"I'll put his details in the book and if the owner comes along, I'll let you know."

"Can't he stay with you?" asked Mr Brown.

"My wife doesn't like dogs," said the policeman.

"No, no," said Mr Brown, "not with you personally. I meant, can't he stay here at the police station?"

"I'm afraid not," said the policeman, shaking his head. "We've only got a couple of cells here, and they're full most of the time. If you can't keep him, you'd better take him along to Battersea Dogs' Home."

"Oh no!" said Hamlet.

"Oh dear!" said Mr Brown.

The policeman said "Oh dear!" as well, but for a different reason. "There seems to be a puddle on the counter, sir."

"Oh dear!" said Mr Brown again. "I am sorry. I think we'd better be going. Hamlet, Susan, come along now."

And leaving a very large puddle and a very unhappy policeman behind them, the Browns and their beagle made hastily for the door.

"Well," said Mr Brown, when they were safely back in the car, "that was a little unfortunate. What are we going to do now?"

"Go home," said Hamlet.

"And it's my turn to hold him," said Susan, grabbing the puppy from Hamlet. He let him go, but said very firmly, "He's mine, he isn't yours."

"The truth is," said Mr Brown, "we don't know who he belongs to. We don't even know what he's called."

"Let's give him a name," said Hamlet.

"Good idea," said Mr Brown. "How about Rover. I've always wanted a Rover – not that I'm unhappy with our Mini!"

"Oh, Dad!" said Susan.

"I know what we should call him," said Hamlet. "We should call him Puddles!"

"That's brilliant," said Mr Brown. "Puddles is perfect. At least he hasn't made one in the car."

"Oh, Dad!" said Susan.

"Oh no!" said Mr Brown.

"Oh yes!" said Hamlet, who decided he'd done the right thing, letting Susan hold the puppy on the journey home.

4. A Witch in Wimbledon

"What on earth are we going to do with this naughty puppy?" said Mrs Brown.

Mr Brown didn't say anything because he was still outside, mopping up the back seat of the car. Susan didn't say anything because she was having a hot bath. Hamlet didn't say anything because he knew his mother didn't want to hear what he had to say.

"I know what you're thinking, Hamlet," she went on, "but we can't keep him."

"Why not, Mum?"

"We just can't."

"But if he goes to Battersea Dogs' Home," Hamlet said with a sigh, "*anything* could happen to him."

"If he goes to Battersea Dogs' Home," said his mother, "someone who wants a beagle will come along and give him a good home."

"I want a beagle," said Hamlet.

"You want to get to bed, my boy," said Mrs Brown.

"Can Puddles come too?"

"No," said Mrs Brown.

"*Please!*" said Hamlet.

"Oh, all right," said Mrs Brown, giving in with a sigh. "Upstairs with you both. We'll sort everything out tomorrow."

When tomorrow came, Hamlet woke up feeling sad. "Today's the day they're going to take Puddles to Battersea Dogs' Home."

Puddles woke up feeling happy. He had spent a cosy night at the foot of Hamlet's bed, and now he was ready for breakfast.

Hamlet was feeling peckish too, which, since it was already half past nine, wasn't very surprising. Hamlet gave Puddles a quick good-morning cuddle and the two friends scampered down to the kitchen.

"Good news, my boy," said Mr Brown, as Hamlet munched into his first bite of toast. "Puddles doesn't have to go to Battersea Dogs' Home after all."

"Yippee!" said Hamlet. "We're going to keep him!"

"No," said Mrs Brown quickly, "we're not going to keep him – but we think we've found his real home."

"Oh," said Hamlet, feeling sadder than ever.

"You can thank Susan," explained Mrs Brown.

"What's Susan got to do with it?" said Hamlet. He didn't like the idea of having to thank Susan for anything.

"Tell your brother what happened, Susan," said Mrs Brown.

"It was like this," said Susan, sitting up at the table and sounding as if she was about to tell everyone a favourite bedtime story.

"Get on with it," hissed Hamlet.

Susan ignored her brother. "It was like this.
You know how I always take all the empty
bottles up the road to the bottle bank on
Sunday morning?"

Hamlet did know.

"Well, when I got there and I'd finished
getting the bottles out of the basket-on-wheels
and was popping them into the bottle bank –"

"Do hurry up," interrupted Hamlet.

"Well," continued Susan, "between the hole where you put the green bottles and the one where you put the white bottles, I found a card."

"What did it say?" asked Hamlet, who was now bursting to find out.

"You can read it for yourself," said Mr Brown, handing Hamlet a grubby-looking piece of yellow card.

LOST: ONE BEAGLE PUPPY

He looks scruffy, but he is very special. If you find him, please telephone 081-201 1948.

"Puddles doesn't look scruffy," said Hamlet.

"But he is a beagle puppy," said Mr Brown. "We'd better give the people a call."

"Can I ring them, Dad?" asked Hamlet,

who had had only one bite of toast, but wasn't
feeling hungry any more.

"OK," said Mr Brown.

Hamlet went over to the telephone with the
card and dialled the number. It rang and rang.

"There's no one there," said Hamlet.

"Keep trying," said Mr Brown.

"Hello," said Hamlet. Someone had

answered. It was a very sleepy man's voice, rough and gruff, and it said, "The King's dead!"

Hamlet put down the receiver. "It was a strange man and he said the King's dead. Do you think it's a secret message?"

"It's very odd," said Mr Brown. "Perhaps you rang the wrong number. Try again."

Hamlet dialled again. This time the telephone was answered straight away. It was the same man, but he was wide awake this time, "The King's dead!"

"Sorry," said Hamlet. "Did you say the King's dead?"

"No," said the voice, "I said the King's Head. This is a pub, but we're not open till eleven. Good morning." And he put down the phone.

"Try once more," said Mr Brown.

Hamlet tried once more. The same man answered. He sounded rougher and gruffer than ever. "What do you want?"

"Have you lost a dog?" Hamlet asked quickly.

"A dog? Have we lost a dog? No, we haven't lost a dog," said the man. Then Hamlet heard somebody talking in the background. "Hold on a minute."

A few seconds later, a woman's voice came on the line. She sounded a lot friendlier. "Sorry about my husband," she said. "We were up very late last night. It's Mrs McGinty you're after. She's lost one of her beagle pups."

"That's right," said Hamlet.

"She's not on the phone, but just come to the King's Head in Wimbledon, and you'll find her place in the alley round the back. You can't miss it."

"Thanks," said Hamlet.

"Not at all," said the woman. "And drop in for a pint while you're about it."

"I will," said Hamlet, who didn't like to tell the lady he was only nine and didn't drink beer. "Thanks."

Hamlet reported the conversation to the family. Mr Brown was very excited.

"The King's Head in Wimbledon," he said. "I know it well. It's just round the corner from the theatre. After rehearsals we sometimes pop in for a pint. They serve some excellent ale. Let's be on our way."

"Can't we leave it till tomorrow?" said Hamlet.

"No," said Mr Brown, lifting his hand in a dramatic gesture. "If it is to be done, 'tis best it were done quickly! Come, boy, come, Puddles, we're off to the King's Head."

As it was Sunday morning there wasn't much traffic, so they reached Wimbledon in about ten minutes. Mr Brown parked the car close to the theatre, so that he could show Hamlet the poster for his pantomime, and then they walked down the road to the pub. Sure enough, at the side of the King's Head there was a narrow alley-way.

"This is it," said Mr Brown.

"Yap, yap," went Puddles, wagging his tail furiously.

Yes, thought Hamlet sadly, this is it.

They walked down the alley-way and came to a high wooden fence with a door in it. Standing on tiptoe, Mr Brown could just see over the fence.

"It's an old stable yard. It's very run-down. There's a couple of horses in one of the stables and there's a goat and there's a chicken and –"

Suddenly the door to the yard opened and a voice said, "Yes?"

Mr Brown and Hamlet found themselves standing face to face with a witch. Of course, she wasn't really a witch, but to Hamlet she

looked like one. She didn't have a pointed hat, but she did have a pointed nose and a pointed chin, and long, bony, pointed fingers. She also had jet-black spiky hair and a spiky sort of voice.

"Have you got Scruff?" she asked.

"Yes," said Mr Brown.

"No," said Hamlet. "We've got Puddles."

Mrs McGinty looked at the puppy. "That's Scruff all right," she said. "Come on in."

Mr Brown and Hamlet and the puppy with two names followed Mrs McGinty into the yard. "Look," she said, "there's his mother."

In one corner of the yard sitting on an old tartan rug outside a large wooden kennel was a fully grown beagle. The moment she saw the puppy she began yapping. Hamlet let go of Puddles and he bounded home to his mother.

"Puddles is a good name for him," said Mrs McGinty. "I've never known a puppy make so many of them. Let's call him Puddles from now on."

Hamlet was beginning to like the witch.

"You can call me Mrs M. My name's McGinty, but everyone calls me Mrs M."

Mr Brown introduced himself and Hamlet, and then told Mrs M the story of how Puddles had turned up in Hamlet's bedroom on Saturday morning. "What I can't understand," said Mr Brown, "is how a puppy could get all the way from Wimbledon to Hammersmith. It's at least six miles."

"I'll tell you what happened," said Mrs M, shooing the chicken away as she took the Browns around the yard. "On Friday night I let Beauty – that's the mother – and the three pups go into the pub. At closing-time, Beauty came home with just two pups. One of the lads in the pub got a bit carried away and decided to take young Scruff – sorry, young Puddles – for a ride. He took him in the basket on the back of his bike, if you please! As you might expect, the poor puppy didn't think much of it and, after about ten minutes,

managed to jump out of the basket and run
off. The lad chased after him, but Puddles
escaped into somebody's garden and that was
that."

"Are you sure that's what happened?"
asked Hamlet.

"That's what the lad told me when he came
back on Saturday morning. He felt very bad
about it – and quite right too. He said Puddles
had run off in Hammersmith, so I gave him

some notices to stick up around the place, in case the puppy turned up."

"And he has!" said Mr Brown. Then he went, "Ow!" and jumped a foot in the air. The goat had nipped Mr Brown's bottom.

"That's Gordon for you. He'll eat anything," said Mrs M. "Sorry."

"That's quite all right," said Mr Brown, who had decided it was time to leave. "I think we'd better be on our way now."

"Can I come and visit Puddles?" asked Hamlet.

"Of course you can," said Mrs M. "Come whenever you like. And bring your dad. I think our Gordon's taken a fancy to him."

5. "Stinging-nettle Soup?"

Hamlet wanted to go and visit Puddles the very next day, but he couldn't. It was Monday and he had to go to school.

"Can I go after school?"

"No," said Mrs Brown firmly. "Wait till the end of term."

"But –" Hamlet protested.

"No buts now," said Mrs Brown. "There are only three more days of term. You'll have homework tonight and tomorrow, and on Wednesday it's the carol concert."

"I can miss that," said Hamlet, who didn't like carol concerts.

"No, you can't," said Mrs Brown. "We're all going. Susan's giving one of the readings."

"Of course she is," said Hamlet, "she's such a goodie-goodie."

"Don't worry," said Mr Brown, "I'll drive

you over to see Puddles on Thursday when I go to my rehearsal."

"Can I come too?" asked Susan.

"You're not invited," said Hamlet. "Mrs M hasn't asked you!"

"It's not Mrs M I want to see," said Susan. "It's Dad's rehearsals."

Susan wanted to be an actor. Susan had wanted to be an actor ever since she was five and had played the part of a sheep in the school nativity play. Mrs Murdoch, who produced the play, had told Mr Brown that Susan was the best sheep she'd ever seen. Susan had been the star attraction in Mrs Murdoch's nativity play for five years running – first as a sheep, then as a shepherd, next as a Wise Man, then as Mary, and finally as the Archangel Gabriel. (Hamlet thought she was particularly soppy as the angel.) Last summer Susan had even acted professionally. She'd had a small part in a play that Mr Brown was in at the Open Air Theatre in Regent's Park.

She had loved every minute of it.

"Can I come and watch your rehearsal, Dad?" she asked.

"Of course you can," said Mr Brown, who always loved having an audience, even an audience of one.

On Thursday, Mr Brown and Hamlet and Susan set off for Wimbledon at half past nine. Mr Brown dropped Hamlet off at the King's Head and went on to the theatre. The pantomime was going to open on Saturday, so today there was to be a full-dress rehearsal.

Mr Brown sat Susan in the middle of the front row of the stalls to watch. Mr Brown was playing the part of Buttons, who loves Cinderella, but loses her when she goes and marries the Prince. Susan thought Mr Brown was far too old to be playing Buttons until she saw the person who was playing Cinderella. She looked as if she was at least thirty.

Susan was eleven and there was a part for an eleven-year-old in the pantomime. The Fairy Godmother, who helps Cinderella go to the ball and meet the Prince, had an assistant fairy and she was played by an eleven-year-old called Sabrina Taylor. That wasn't the girl's real name, it was her stage name.

Sabrina Taylor was at stage school, which was how she'd got the part in the pantomime. Susan would have liked to go to stage school, but Mrs Brown didn't think it was a good idea.

Susan couldn't understand how Sabrina Taylor had got the part of the assistant fairy, because she felt a fairy should be fair and pretty and light on her feet, and Sabrina was, well, to put it bluntly, fat. Not only was she fat, but she had frizzy ginger hair and a horrid high squeaky voice.

Even though she thought Cinderella was too old and the assistant fairy was too fat, Susan had a very happy day in the stalls at the Wimbledon Theatre. And Hamlet had a very happy day in the stables behind the King's Head.

"I've been expecting you," said Mrs M, when Hamlet first put his head around the yard door. "Come on in."

"How's Puddles?" asked Hamlet.

"He's as happy as a hedgehog," said Mrs M. "Take a look."

Hamlet went over to the kennel, where Puddles was busy playing a game of hide-and-seek with his mother's old tartan rug.

"Hello, Puddles," said Hamlet. "Do you remember me?"

Puddles looked up and yapped a friendly greeting.

"Since you're here, young man," Mrs M said to Hamlet, "would you mind lending me a hand?"

Normally Hamlet wasn't too keen on work, but when Mrs McGinty asked, it seemed different somehow.

"What do you want me to do?" he asked.

"I'll show you," said Mrs M.

She led Hamlet in the stable where she kept her two horses. "This one's called Sarah and the little one's called Susan. Nice names, aren't they?"

Hamlet didn't say anything.

"Now what we've got to do is muck out the stable, shift all the dirty straw and put down clean stuff. It's hard work."

And it was. It was made even harder by Puddles, who kept getting in the way.

"Can you ride?" asked Mrs M.

"I don't know," said Hamlet, "I've never tried." That wasn't quite true. He had tried once, but he'd fallen off. Susan, of course, was a very good rider, which was the other reason Hamlet hadn't wanted to get back on to a horse.

"I give riding lessons on the Common on Saturday mornings," said Mrs M. "I'll give you a free one to get you started."

It was funny to think that the person who seemed to be a frightening witch when Hamlet first set eyes on her turned out to be a friendly riding teacher.

At half past twelve, Mrs M said, "Time for lunch. I've made some nettle soup."

"Stinging-nettle soup?" said Hamlet nervously, thinking she was perhaps a witch after all.

"Yes, but it won't sting you. It's delicious. Try some."

"No, thanks," said Hamlet. "That's very nice of you, but my dad gave me some money for a hamburger. I'll go and get it now."

The hamburger restaurant was only two doors down from the King's Head, and Hamlet was back in five minutes with a quarter-pounder and cheese and a large portion of chips.

When he got back to the yard, he couldn't see Mrs M. The horses were there and the goat and the chicken, and Puddles and his family, but there was no sign of Mrs McGinty.

"Where's she gone?" Hamlet wondered.

He put down his hamburger and chips and looked in the horses' stable. She wasn't there. He looked in the next stable, which belonged to Gordon, and she wasn't there either. He hadn't been inside the third stable before. As he opened the door he called out, "Mrs M, are you there?"

There was no reply. He went in and was surprised to find that this stable wasn't really a stable at all. There was a large rug on the cobble-stone floor, and two big old armchairs and a kitchen table. There was even an old gas cooker next to a proper sink.

"Hello, Hamlet," said Mrs M.

Hamlet almost jumped out of his skin. Where was she? He could hear her voice, but he couldn't see her. So she was a witch after all!

"Mrs M," he said nervously, backing towards the door. "Where are you?"

"I'm here," said the voice.

"Where?" said Hamlet.

"Up here!" said Mrs M.

Hamlet looked up towards the ceiling and there was Mrs M, sitting on a narrow ledge that ran along one side of the stable wall.

"This is my bedroom," she said with a chuckle. "I'd invite you up but there's only room for me and the mattress."

"How do you get up there?" asked Hamlet, who couldn't believe that anyone would choose to sleep on a mattress on a shelf, three-quarters of the way up a stable wall.

"Guess?" said Mrs M.

"You use a ladder," said Hamlet, even though he couldn't see one.

"No."

"You fly?" said Hamlet, who was beginning to believe she *really* was a witch.

"No," said Mrs M.

"I give up," said Hamlet.

"I use this," said Mrs M, throwing a thick rope off the edge of the ledge. It landed by Hamlet's feet, and moments later that's where Mrs M was as well. She swung off the mattress on the rope, and lowered herself quickly to the ground.

"It's the only way to travel," said Mrs M. "Beats a broomstick every time," she added with a wink. "You see, I read minds too."

Hamlet felt himself go a little red. He

didn't know what to say.

"Are you sure you won't have any of my nettle soup?" asked Mrs M.

"No, thanks," said Hamlet quickly. "I've got my hamburger. I'll go and get it."

Hamlet ran out into the yard and arrived just in time to witness Gordon the goat polishing off the quarter-pounder and cheese, wrapping-paper and all. There was no sign of the chips either. Gordon had obviously had them as a starter.

Nettle soup, here I come, thought Hamlet, as he returned to Mrs M in the stable. "I'm afraid Gordon's eaten my lunch, so –"

"Don't worry," said Mrs M, "you don't have to have the nettle soup. I expect Lady Godiva will be able to help you."

"Lady Godiva," said Hamlet. "Wasn't she . . . ?"

"Now close your eyes," said Mrs M. "Take my hand and follow me."

She *is* a witch, thought Hamlet, but he did

as he was told. He could tell they were leaving Mrs M's stable and crossing the yard. They seemed to be going into another stable, a much darker one and very smelly.

"Now," said Mrs M, "open your eyes and meet Lady Godiva."

Hamlet opened his eyes and found himself face to face with the chicken.

"And look," said Mrs M with a laugh, "she's sitting on your lunch."

6. First-Night Nerves

Lady Godiva very generously provided
Hamlet with two eggs for his lunch on
Thursday and with two more on Friday. She
didn't seem to be in an egg-laying mood on
Saturday, so Hamlet bravely tried the nettle
soup and found it was delicious.

All in all, Hamlet spent three of the happiest
days he could remember in Mrs McGinty's
back yard. Mrs Brown had always found it
next to impossible to persuade Hamlet to
sweep out the kitchen at Number 13, but Mrs
M had no trouble at all in getting Hamlet to
muck out the stables at the King's Head.

At the end of the day on Thursday and
Friday, Mr Brown and Susan had come to
collect Hamlet on their way home from
rehearsals. On Saturday night it was different.

Saturday night was the first night of

Cinderella at the Wimbledon Theatre, so at a quarter to seven Hamlet said goodbye to Mrs M and to Puddles and his friends at the stables, and set off on the short walk to the theatre. He had arranged to meet his mother and sister by the ticket office. Sure enough, there they were, though he hardly recognized them, they were both looking so elegant in their best first-night clothes. Hamlet was looking the way you'd expect a nine-year-old to look after he's spent the day mucking out two horses, a goat, a dog, three puppies and a chicken.

Mrs Brown had three tickets in her hand and butterflies in her stomach. She was always nervous on first nights, even if she wasn't in the play herself. She was sure someone would forget their lines or fall over the scenery.

"Don't look so worried, Mum," said Susan, who had seen three dress rehearsals by now. "If Dad falls over the scenery, he'll be doing it on purpose." Then she added in a rather loud whisper, "Dad's great, but Cinderella's a bit old, and the girl playing the Fairy Godmother's assistant is hopeless."

"Oh dear," said Mrs Brown.

A voice came over the loudspeaker in the foyer. "Ladies and gentlemen, kindly take your seats as tonight's performance of *Cinderella* is about to commence."

The Browns made their way to their seats – Mr Brown had got them the best, in the centre of the stalls, at the front – and they settled down to enjoy the show.

The lights in the theatre dimmed, the orchestra began to play, and the curtain went up to reveal a magical fairy glade bathed in moonlight. Sitting on a giant toadstool was the Fairy Godmother, all in sparkling silver, and standing at her side was her plump, ginger-headed assistant, dressed in very bright pink. Skipping about the stage were lots of other children, playing younger fairies.

When the music stopped, the Fairy Godmother waved her magic wand and said, "Come, fairies, gather round. Tonight is a night when dreams come true and we have spells to cast and work to do. There is a fair young girl called Cinderella, who is out gathering firewood in the forest. She needs our help and we must find her. Sweetpea, you will lead the way."

Sweetpea was the plump, red-headed assistant fairy. In her squeaky voice, she said, "I will do so, Fairy Godmother – without delay."

And without delay, Sweetpea led the way. Unfortunately, it was the wrong way. It was the first night and Sweetpea was very nervous. The lights were so bright, Sweetpea couldn't really see where she was going – so she skipped down the stage and straight over the edge, into the orchestra pit.

The poor Fairy Godmother darted after her assistant and tried to grab her. But Sweetpea was tubby and the Fairy Godmother was tiny, and, as Sweetpea fell off the stage, the Fairy Godmother fell too.

The little fairies left on the stage all screamed. People in the audience screamed. Musicians in the orchestra screamed. Sweetpea and the Fairy Godmother screamed – and with good reason.

Almost at once the lights in the theatre came up, the curtain on the stage came down, and usherettes appeared from nowhere. The theatre manager marched on to the stage and called to the audience, "Is there a doctor in the house?"

The lady sitting immediately in front of Hamlet stood up. It was Dr Lo from Hammersmith. She made her way along her row and down the aisle. By now a violinist and a trombone player had helped the wounded fairies out of the orchestra pit, and Dr Lo joined them as they hobbled through a

door at the far side of the theatre.

"If you will bear with me, ladies and gentlemen, boys and girls," said the theatre manager, "I'll just find out what's happening."

"Oh dear," said Mrs Brown, for the second time that evening. "I do so hate first nights."

The theatre manager was already back on the stage. "Good news, ladies and gentlemen, boys and girls, our Fairy Godmother and her assistant are now in the hands of an excellent doctor, and the show can go on!"

Everyone in the audience (except Mrs

Brown) gave a cheer and clapped their hands.

"I hope you will understand," continued the theatre manager, "that for the rest of tonight's performance, the part of the Fairy Godmother will have to be played by one of the stage management, who will read the words from a book."

Fortunately, the part of the Fairy Godmother was not a big one and she wasn't due to appear again for quite a few scenes. So by the time a tall, dark-haired stagehand in jeans and a T-shirt came on, holding a copy of the script, the audience were so enjoying themselves that it didn't really matter.

Everything else about the pantomime was just right. The music was wonderful, the scenery was spectacular, and the way the pumpkin and the two white mice were turned into a crystal carriage drawn by ponies was so magical, it really took your breath away. Mrs Brown and Hamlet didn't think Cinderella was too old, and even Susan had to admit she

74

was an excellent singer and dancer.

The best thing in the show, of course, was Mr Brown as Buttons. He was very funny, and when he bumped into the scenery (which he did a lot), you knew he was doing it on purpose. Both Hamlet and Susan thought Cinderella was making a serious mistake marrying the Prince, when she could have married Buttons.

Everyone must have liked Buttons, because at the end of the show when he came on to take his bow, he got the loudest cheer. The second loudest cheer went to the stagehand in the jeans and T-shirt.

"What did you think?" asked a beaming Mr Brown, as he welcomed Hamlet and Susan and Mrs Brown into his dressing-room.

"Brilliant, Dad!" said Hamlet and Susan together.

"You were marvellous, darling," said Mrs Brown, and she meant it.

"Thank you all!" said Mr Brown, taking an

extra bow. "I'd like to propose a toast, if I
may," he added, popping open a bottle of
champagne and pouring some into four paper
cups that he had laid out on the dressing-
table. "Here's to the best audience in the
world! Cheers!"

"Cheers!" said Hamlet and Susan,
pretending to sip the champagne. (They liked
the idea, but they hated the taste.)

"And shouldn't we drink a toast to the poor
Fairy Godmother and her assistant?"
suggested Mrs Brown.

"Yes, indeed," said Mr Brown merrily,
taking another gulp of champagne.

"How are they, Dad?" asked Susan.

"Not too well, I'm afraid," said Mr Brown,
putting down his paper cup. "The Fairy
Godmother has put her back out, poor dear,
and is bent double, and little Sweetpea, bless
her, has sprained her ankle. They'll both be
off for at least a week."

"Oh dear," said Mrs Brown for the third
time that evening. "What a disaster!"

"Not really," said Mr Brown, helping
himself to a little more champagne. "We've
found replacements for them both already."

"Already?"

"At least," said Mr Brown, with a wicked

twinkle in his eye, "I *think* we've found replacements."

"Oh, no . . ." said Mrs Brown, looking alarmed.

"Oh, yes . . ." chuckled Mr Brown, looking his wife straight in the eye.

7. What a Pantomime!

"My darling, *you* are going to be our Fairy Godmother!" announced Mr Brown.

"Oh, no I'm not," said Mrs Brown.

"Oh, yes you are," said Mr Brown.

"Oh, no I'm not!" said Mrs Brown.

"And *you*," said Mr Brown, turning to Susan, "you, my sweet daughter, are going to be your darling mother's Sweetpea!"

"Oh, yes, Dad," said Susan. "Come on, Mum."

"No," said Mrs Brown. "I'm sorry. I can't do it. I won't do it."

"Not even if a prince went down on bended knee and asked you?" said a handsome young man who had just put his head round Mr Brown's dressing-room door.

"It's Prince Charming," said Susan.

"At your service, Miss Sweetpea," said the

Prince, giving Susan a royal bow.

Between them Mr Brown and Prince Charming, who was also the pantomime's director, persuaded Mrs Brown that she had to save the day and play the part. Susan, of course, didn't need any persuading.

On Sunday, Number 13 Irving Terrace, Hammersmith, was deserted. All four members of the Brown family were in Wimbledon. Hamlet was enjoying another busy day in the stables behind the King's Head. (Mrs McGinty had persuaded Lady Godiva to provide another splendid lunch.) Mr Brown was watching Susan and Mrs Brown rehearse on the stage of the Wimbledon Theatre. Under the direction of Prince Charming, and with enthusiastic advice from Buttons, the Fairy Godmother and Sweetpea went over their scenes again and again.

By Monday lunchtime they had learnt all their lines and knew all their moves, but they were still very nervous when they climbed into their costumes for the first time. Mrs Brown's costume was far too small for her. Susan's was far too big.

"This is your first night," said Mr Brown, putting his head round the door of the dressing-room Susan and her mother were sharing. "Good luck!"

"I hate first nights," said Mrs Brown.

It was Christmas Eve and the theatre was packed. There wasn't a single seat to spare, so when Hamlet arrived to see the performance, the theatre manager took him backstage. "I'm afraid you'll have to watch the show from the wings."

Hamlet didn't mind at all. It was much more exciting to be seeing the show from the side of the stage than the centre of the stalls.

"I'm not in the way, am I?" Hamlet asked the stagehand in the jeans and T-shirt.

"Not at all," she said, "but you'll have to

move when the ponies come on."

"Where are they?" asked Hamlet.

"They're in a horse-box in the car-park out
the back. We bring them in at the interval so
that they're ready to begin the Second Act. I'll
tell you when you've got to move."

"Thanks," said Hamlet.

"Ladies and gentlemen," said the voice on the loudspeaker. "Kindly take your seats as tonight's performance of *Cinderella* is about to commence."

Mrs Brown and Susan and all the younger fairies were already in position on stage. Mrs Brown caught sight of Hamlet in the wings and gave him a little wave.

I hope I'm not going to put her off, he thought as he waved back. Suddenly there was no more time for thinking. The orchestra was playing, the curtain was going up, the stage was flooded with moonlight, and Hamlet could hear his mother saying loud and clear, "Come, fairies, gather round. Tonight is a night when dreams come true . . ."

It was obvious straight away that Mrs Brown was miles better than the other Fairy Godmother. And even Hamlet could see that Susan was a lot better than Sabrina Taylor. What's more, when Susan led the little fairies

off the stage, she knew where she was going.

When the interval came, everyone was feeling happy. The show was going well.

"Time to fetch the ponies," said the stagehand in the jeans and T-shirt. Hamlet got off his stool. "You can come with me if you like."

Hamlet followed the stagehand to the back of the wings, where there was a large metal door with a green sign above it saying FIRE EXIT. The stagehand pushed open the door and the pair of them walked down a short ramp that led to the car-park.

"The horse-box is just back here," said the stagehand, taking Hamlet round the side of the building. "That's funny," she said, pointing to a large empty parking-space. "This is where the horse-box is supposed to be. Where's it gone? Joe can't have moved it."

Joe hadn't moved it. He hadn't brought it at all. On Saturday night, he had taken the horse-box and the ponies back to the farm

where they belonged. He'd planned to leave
them there till Wednesday, which was Boxing
Day. There was no performance on Sunday
because it was Sunday. There was no
performance on Tuesday because it was
Christmas Day. Joe was sure there was no
performance on Monday either. Joe was
wrong.

The stagehand was frantic. "Panic stations!" she said. "We've got no ponies. If it's not one disaster, it's another!" She rushed back into the theatre to spread the bad news.

"Help! We've lost the ponies!"

"Oh dear!" said Mrs Brown, who had just begun to relax.

"The show must go on!" said Mr Brown. "I know what we'll do."

"What?" said the stagehand.

"We'll dress you up as a pony!"

"Oh dear," said Mrs Brown.

"Come on, let's see what we've got in Wardrobe."

"Wardrobe" was what Mr Brown called the tiny dressing-room where all the spare costumes were kept. The person who looked after the costumes was the wardrobe mistress, and when Mr Brown and the stagehand arrived, they found her mending one of the younger fairy's wings.

"No time for repairs, I'm afraid," said Mr

Brown, charging into the room. "We need a pony costume – and quickly!"

"A pony costume?" said the wardrobe mistress, adding the final stitch to the fairy's wing. "I'm afraid I can't help you there. I've got a lovely *cow* costume. Would that do?"

"I think it'll have to!" said Mr Brown with a sigh.

Over the loudspeaker the message came: "Ladies and gentlemen, please take your seats. The Second Act of *Cinderella* is about to commence."

The stagehand in the jeans and T-shirt climbed into the front of the cow costume and Prince Charming climbed into the back. The wardrobe mistress zipped them in, and Mr Brown led them towards the stage, declaring, "Cinderella shall go to the ball – in a crystal coach, drawn by a cow!"

When the curtain went up on the Second Act of *Cinderella*, nobody in the audience knew that anything was wrong. They were full of

interval ice-creams and Christmas cheer, and
were looking forward happily to the rest of the
show.

There were Buttons and Cinderella in the
kitchen at Hardup Hall, and there was the
Fairy Godmother telling Cinderella that
tonight her dreams would come true and she
would go to the Prince's Ball.

90

"You'll need a coach to take you there, my dear," said Mrs Brown. "Do you happen to have a pumpkin close at hand?"

Mr Brown found the pumpkin by the fireplace and showed it to the Fairy Godmother.

"Good. That's exactly what I need." She waved her magic wand, there was a flash, and a piece of scenery was lifted into the air to reveal a shimmering crystal coach. The audience clapped.

"You'll need ponies to pull your carriage," said the Fairy Godmother, sounding just a little uncertain for the first time that evening. "Do you have any nice white mice?"

Mr Brown showed the Fairy Godmother the cage containing the two mice. (They were made of sugar, but to the audience they looked like real white mice.)

"Excellent," said Mrs Brown. As she lifted her wand, she turned to the audience and whispered loudly, "I ought to warn you, this spell doesn't always work as well as it should."

Mrs Brown crossed her fingers and waved her wand. There was a flash of light, and on to the stage trotted the stagehand and Prince Charming in the cow costume. The audience rolled about laughing. Cinderella and the Fairy Godmother didn't know what to do or

say – and then the cow's udders fell off.

The audience roared. They were having a wonderful time.

Mrs Brown turned to them and shouted, "I warned you the spell doesn't always work."

"Oh, yes it does," the audience shouted back.

"Oh, no it doesn't!" called Mrs Brown.

"Oh, yes it does!" cried the audience happily.

"Oh, very well," said Mrs Brown. "I'll try one more time."

Mrs Brown waved her wand once more, the lights flashed for the last time, and on to the stage of the Wimbledon Theatre stepped Hamlet Brown and Mrs McGinty, leading a pair of the prettiest ponies you have ever seen.

The audience cheered and cheered.

By the time the show had ended and the cheering had stopped, and the Browns had taken off their costumes and walked to the

King's Head with Mrs M and her ponies, it
was very late indeed.

It was after midnight when the Browns got
back to Number 13. When Hamlet clambered
into bed, he was tired, but very happy. It had

been an exciting day and tomorrow – well, later today, really – it would be Christmas.

Hamlet didn't wake up until after nine o'clock. He wouldn't have woken up then if he hadn't been having this extraordinary dream. Hamlet dreamt he was being eaten by a cow. He woke up and there, sitting on the pillow, licking Hamlet's face and making snuffly noises in his ear, was Puddles. He had a red ribbon round his neck and a little note tied to it: "Happy Christmas, Hamlet, with lots of love from Mummy and Daddy and Mrs M."